TED'S GREAT SPACE ADVENTURE

ELIZABETH AVERY

ROYAL
OBSERVATORY
GREENWICH

Ted is no ordinary teddy bear.
Ted is an explorer.

Ted often sneaks off on super-duper-megamassive adventures. One night Ted decided to have a nice cup of teddy tea, a biscuit and a good long think about the next adventure.

Gazing out of the window Ted thought, "The night sky looks so beautiful! The planets and stars look like twinkly sky diamonds."

"I like that one," Ted said, pointing to the sky. "No, that one! No, wait – that one! Oh, I don't know, I can't decide!" said Ted, with a big bear huff. Choosing a favourite can be a very tricky business.

Suddenly, a great big bear brainwave came to Ted. "Jiggling jellyfish, I've got it! My next adventure will be a trip through our solar system!"

Ted jumped aboard the rocket and zipped up the most fancy-pants space suit you could ever imagine.

BEEP, CHIRP, BOOP!

Ursa, the on-board computer, sprang into life.

"Hello, Ted! Where are we going today?"

"Ursa, we are going into space to see all the planets round our sun so I can pick my favourite," said Ted.

"Well, in that case, Ted, fasten your seatbelt."

ZIP, CLICK, POP

Ted took a big deep breath then fired up the engines.

The rocket's boosters rumbled into action like a hungry bear belly.

"No adventure can start without a countdown!" shouted Ted over the roar of the engines.

BEAR
BLAST
OFF!'

Whoosh...

. . . they were off!

"Ted, do you want to start with somewhere hot or cold?" asked Ursa.

"Oooooooh, somewhere hot, please, Ursa – I'm feeling tropical!"

"No problem, Ted. I'll take us somewhere close to the Sun – it might get a little toasty though!"

"Yikes! Not too close, we don't want to roast!" said Ted.

OOSH...

The rocket zoomed through space towards Mercury.

"Mercury is the smallest of all the planets in our solar system," said Ursa. "You could fit 16 of them inside Planet Earth."

"Wow! I could race round Mercury in my space buggy super quickly. I think this is my favourite planet!" said Ted excitedly.

"Hold your horses, Ted! We need to see the others before you decide which one you like best!" bleeped Ursa.

WHOOSH...

Next up on the adventure was Venus.
"Venus is the hottest planet in the Solar System,
because a thick layer of gas around it traps all the
heat in like a greenhouse," said Ursa.

"This has got to be my favourite planet! I love going
to hot places on holiday!" squeaked Ted.

"The temperature on Venus can get to a scorching
470°C. It's even hotter than super-sausage-sizzling
temperature!" Ursa bleeped.

"Sausage-sizzling temperature?! Eeek! I want to eat sausages, not sizzle like them," said Ted. "Let's get off this planet!!"

WHOOSH...

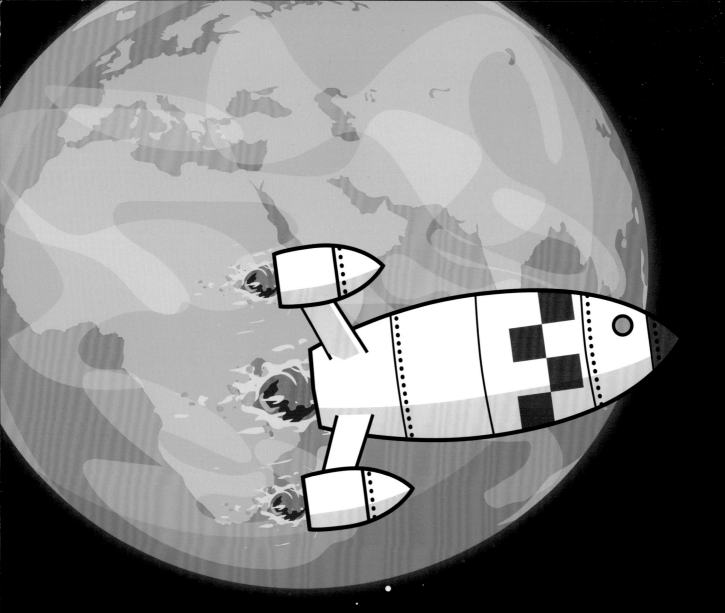

"Next up on our solar system tour is Planet Earth!
You already know quite a lot about this planet, because
we live there!" said Ursa.

"Look how beautiful it is from up here!" said Ted,
peering out of the rocket at Earth's deep blue oceans,
lush green forests and stunning sandy deserts.

"What is that?" asked Ted, pointing to the side of
Earth.

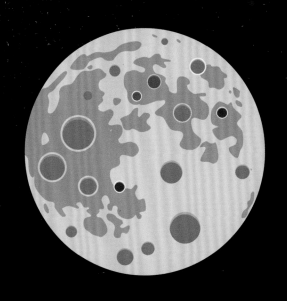

"That is our moon, Ted. The Moon is smaller than Earth and covered in dents called craters where space rocks have smashed into it over the years," Ursa explained.

"Ooooh, it looks beautiful. An adventure for another time perhaps."

WHOOSH...

The next stop was Mars.

"Robots called rovers have been busy exploring Mars for quite some time! They send photographs back to Earth so scientists understand more about Mars," Ursa told Ted.

"There's one there," squealed Ted.
"Hello, Rover!"

"There's a giant extinct volcano on Mars called Olympus Mons. It's the biggest volcano in the whole Solar System," Ursa said to Ted over the radio.

"Bouncing bumblebees! I love volcanoes! This planet is my favourite!" said Ted.

WHOOSH...

The adventurers set off again. Ted's rocket began the bumpy journey through the asteroid belt.

"Yikes! Hold on!" Ted said as the rocket zig-zagged through the jumble of asteroids. At last, they left the asteroid belt and a huge planet came into view.

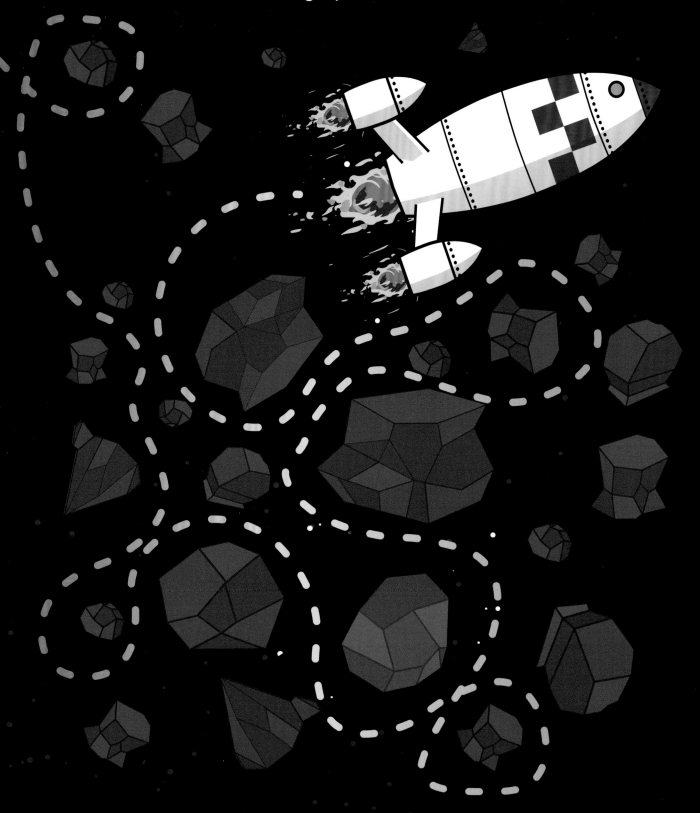

This is Jupiter. It's called a gas giant and is the biggest planet in our solar system," bleeped Ursa. "It is made of gas so you can't stand on the surface – you would fall straight through. It's also super stormy."

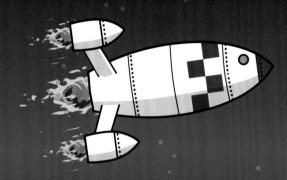

Ted looked down at the huge colourful bands of swirling gas.

"Ooh, I love storms! Jupiter is definitely my favourite!" clapped Ted.

"Hold on, Ted. The storms on Jupiter can be quite scary. There is a storm on Jupiter's surface that's bigger than two planet Earths. It's called the Great Red Spot," said Ursa.

Ted decided that didn't sound like much fun so fired up the rocket's engines again.

WHOOSH...

The next planet they saw was Saturn, the second-largest planet in the Solar System.

"Saturn is made of gas and if you put it in a bubble bath, it would float! You would have to find a big enough bath though!" Ursa told Ted. "Saturn's rings are made of rock and ice."

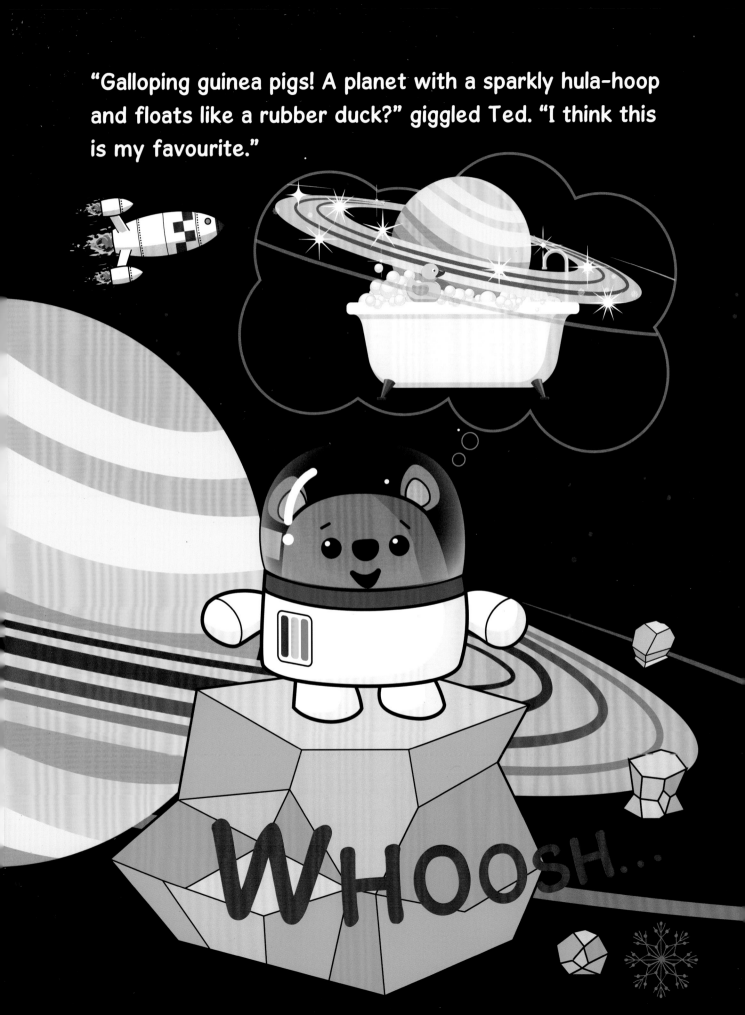

"Galloping guinea pigs! A planet with a sparkly hula-hoop and floats like a rubber duck?" giggled Ted. "I think this is my favourite."

WHOOSH...

The next planet was Uranus.

"Uranus spins on its side rather than upright like the other planets," bleeped Ursa. "Astronomers think it might have been knocked over a very long time ago and just stayed moving sideways instead."

"A funky mover – I like it," squeaked Ted with a giggle and started to break out a few funky moves too! "Perhaps this could be my favourite? It's so cool."

"Come on, Ted. We better get a move on if we're going to see all the planets!" said Ursa.

WHOOSH...

Next they visited Neptune.

"Neptune is a gas giant too and has
the fastest winds in the
Solar System," said Ursa.

"Perfect!" yelped Ted, bouncing
with excitement. "I could
fly my kite there – this is my
favourite for sure!"

"Actually, the wind here is ten times faster than the fastest cars on Earth. We don't want you to blow away!" said Ursa.

"Hopping hamsters – no, we don't!" squeaked Ted.

WHOOSH...

"Ursa, what's that over there?"
asked Ted.

"That's Pluto. It is a dwarf planet.
The temperature on Pluto can be
as low as −240°C. Its surface is
covered in ice," explained Ursa.

"I love ice skating! I definitely
like Pluto," said Ted.

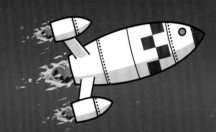

WHOOSH...

"You've been around the whole Solar System now, Ted. Do you have a favourite planet?" quizzed Ursa. "They are all my favourites!" sighed Ted, flinging both paws into the air. "Let's head home for a nice cup of teddy tea and think about it." The rocket whizzed around and headed for home.

As they got closer and closer to home, Ted could see Planet Earth through the window of the rocket.

"Do you know Ursa, I think I've chosen my favourite," said Ted confidently. "Planet Earth!"

Ted gazed at Earth all the way home.
It was definitely the best planet.

As the rocket landed, the Sun was about to rise. It had been a busy day so it was time Ted went to bed.

Ted pulled on a super-snuggly pair of teddy pyjamas and gave a big bear yawn before drifting off into a deep sleep. Ted dreamt of all of the wonderful places they had been and amazing things they had seen in the brilliant Solar System. What an adventure it had been!

WHAT'S YOUR FAVOURITE PLANET?

First published in 2020
by Royal Museums Greenwich,
Park Row, Greenwich, London SE10 9NF

ISBN: 978-1-906367-67-1

© National Maritime Museum, London

At the heart of the UNESCO World Heritage Site of Maritime Greenwich are the four world-class attractions of Royal Museums Greenwich – the National Maritime Museum, the Royal Observatory, the Queen's House and *Cutty Sark*.

www.rmg.co.uk

A CIP catalogue record for this book is available
from the British Library.

Designed by Rich Carr, Carr Design Studio

Printed and bound in the UK by Gomer Press

10 9 8 7 6 5 4 3 2 1